Our Beach Camping Ground

Carmel Reilly

Photographs by
Lindsay Edwards

Contents

Camping by the Beach

Our family likes to go camping every year.
We always stay at a camping ground by the beach.

A Map of Our Beach Camping Ground

We like this camping ground
because it is a good place
to have a holiday.
Lots of our friends go there, too.

The Office

When we get to the camping ground, the first thing we see is the **office**. Emma, from the office, shows us where we can set up our tent.

The **store** is beside the office. We can buy food and drinks at the store.

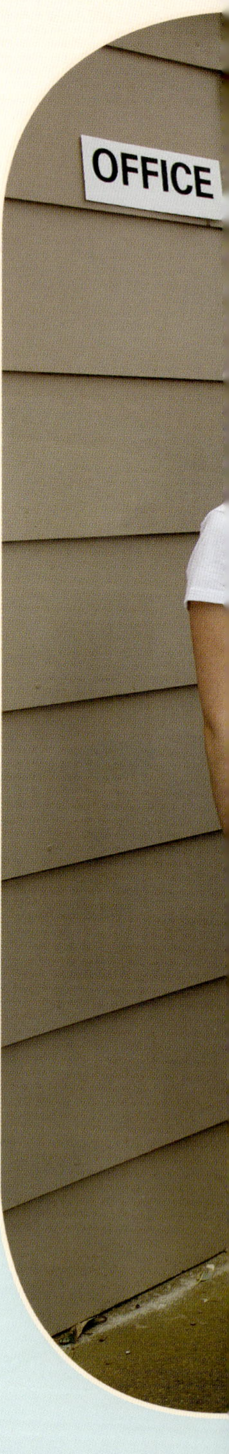

STOP

Setting Up

We drive down a small road
to our camping spot.
It is a good place
for us to set up our tent
and park our car.

We have lots of other tents
all around us.
There are **caravans** near us, too.

Cabins

People who do not have tents or caravans can stay in **cabins**.

Cabins look like small houses.
They have kitchens,
and bathrooms and bedrooms.

There are six cabins
in our camping ground.
They are by the office.

Places to Eat and Wash

The camping ground
has some more buildings, too.

There are two big bathrooms.
One bathroom is near our tent.
The other one is across the road
by the caravans.

The kitchen is in the middle
of the camping ground.

Playing

Children love this camping ground
because there are lots of places to play.
There is a games room
and a playground.
There is a swimming pool, too.

We go to these places every day
to play with our friends.

The Beach

The camping ground
is near the beach.
It only takes five minutes
to walk from our tent
to the water.

Mum and Dad take us to the beach
every morning to swim and play.

Our beach camping ground
is a great place for a holiday.

I love going there
with my family every year.

Glossary

cabins small houses

caravans holiday homes on wheels

office a building for work

store a shop